" WHEN THE STARS GO OUT IS DEDICATED
AND BEAUTIFUL STARS I WAS BLESSED TO BE THE GUARDIAN OF
AT FEATHERSTALE CHILDREN'S VILLAGE TANZANIA. "

JOHN ST JULIEN, FOUNDER AND BABA OF FEATHERSTALE CHILDREN'S VILLAGE

THE PROCEEDS FROM THIS BOOK GO TOWARDS SUPPORTING OUR
EVER - GROWING FAMILY OF NEARLY 200 CHILDREN IN NEED
WHO STILL LIVE IN THE VILLAGE.

WWW. SHARETANZANIA. COM

High up in the dark twinkles of the night sky above,

lived a big lonely star needing a lesson in love.

The star had seen many things,
he had done many things too,

but he just never understood love
like we are supposed to.

The Star was alone, you see,
in that dark corner of space,
and when it comes to making friends,
that's not a great place.

His star heart was okay;
it was so full of twinkling starry love,

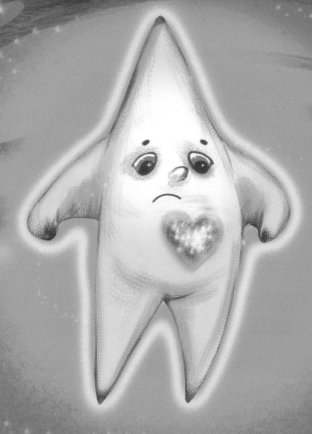

But with no one around him,
he just did not feel as he should of.

Then one dark starry night
with the slimmest of cosmic chance,

Three small lights appeared,
and they began to shimmer and dance.

Those tiny lights grew brighter and more blinding with each passing day

and in time that lonely star and they began to laugh, love and play.

Oh, how happy he was
in the company he now had,

oh, how they all loved each other,
and that made them quite glad!

Before long, the big star became grateful in his corner of space,

It was no longer dull; in fact, it had become a wondrous place!

Then one day,
with the playful curiosity of a cat,
One little star asked a question,
and so began a long chat.

Where is it that we come from big shining star,
was it over there?

Is it over here?

Or is it so far?"

"Well, if I am open, I am not all that sure,
But I believe,
it is a place full of love and ever so pure."

Will we three stars ever go back there and see such a place?"

To which a big wide smile spread across the big stars star face,

"Oh yes,
I am sure that we will, that we can, and we do!

For even here,
I can feel that place inside of me and inside of you,"

and so I just feel
that beyond this dark mysterious sky
is a place we all come from
and go when we say goodbye.

If something as beautiful
as you three came from there,

"I can say" it must be more magical
than our star minds can bear.

The three stars smiled,
content with what they had heard.

In their hearts,
they felt love as their smiles turned inward.

As time did go by,
those four stars had the greatest of fun,

they laughed, and they played,
and their blinding bright star beams did run!

And that big lonely star
whose heart had started out so lost and dull

was finally feeling whole and complete,
and all in all so full.

Finally, the big star had learned
the lesson that we all must.

That having friends and loving others
is more precious than stardust.

Their lives were so content
as they twinkled in the night,

it seemed an end to their joy

was never in sight.

Those 3 little stars
how they shone brighter than most,

shining so bright
Like some sort of angelic cosmic signpost.

Then, on the darkest of nights,
totally out of the blue,

there was a change in the three stars,
and the big star, well, he had no idea what to do.

It began with a crackle,

a fizz,

and a pop.

The big star tried everything to make it stop.

But the light of the three little stars was no longer so whole

and eventually, their once bright star lights faded to dull.

"Little stars! Please!
Why is it that your light is suddenly so low!?"

"We don't know big star, we really don't know,
we just no longer have the strength to glow."

The three stars grew dimmer,
and now only their dullness did grow.
Then one little star whispered,
"I think it is our time to go..."

Then with the last of their rays,
on the big stars star face,
the three stars stopped talking,
stopped shining and lighting up the day with their grace,

And just like that,
those three beautiful stars went away.

The big star was alone,
oh how he wished they could stay.

Oh, how he missed them,
the smiles, laughs, and play
Oh, how he hoped to see them
again someday.

He took time to speak to them
toward that big star-filled sky,
And he listened intently
in the hope of a reply,

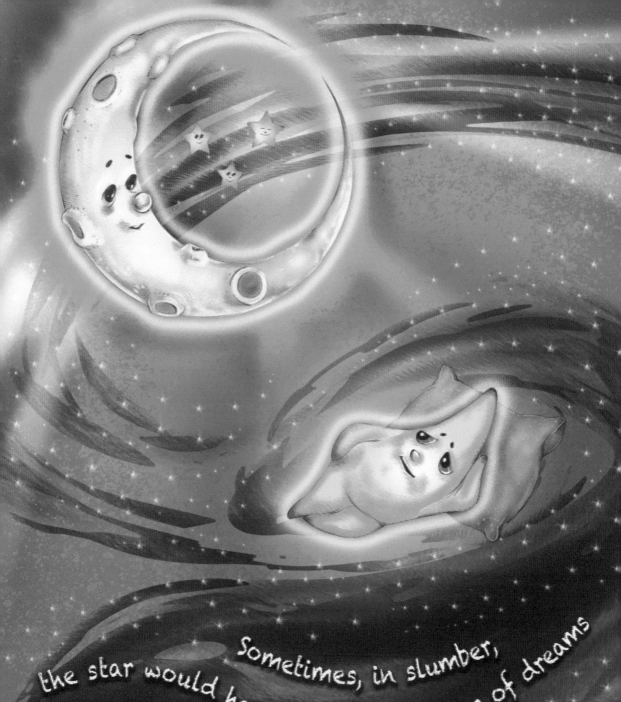

Sometimes, in slumber,
the star would have the most precious of dreams
Then think of the three stars
as he gazed at the moon and its beams.

It was hard for a while
without his three friends

But the love they had shared
began to make amends.

As time went by,
he slowly became a little less sad,

for he remembered with gratitude

all the fun times that they had all had.

Then one sleepy twinkling night
in his dark corner of space,
came an unfamiliar voice
from an unfamiliar face.

Hurtling by with a vast trail of great shining light, was a meteor, a shooting star that lit up the night.

The shooting star shouted
as his trail of light was passing by,
like a pianist playing a tune
while flying through that night sky.

"Hey there, big star,
is you here all alone!?"

Came from his cheery face, all made of stone.

"Well,
it might look like I am as you fly on by here,
but I have a story for you
before you disappear.

Do you see those three white lights,
silently shining and still?

For the most magical of times,
we all had such a thrill!

And for all they are not here
to laugh, smile and play,
they are with me in my heart every single day."

"If those stars are not with you,
then where did they go!?"

Well, to be honest, I really do not know...

But I can tell you this,
that by now I am quite sure...
They are happy where they are
in a place filled with love that is ever so pure.

Printed in Great Britain
by Amazon

19192975R00027